SPRINGS

by Mary J. Guhl

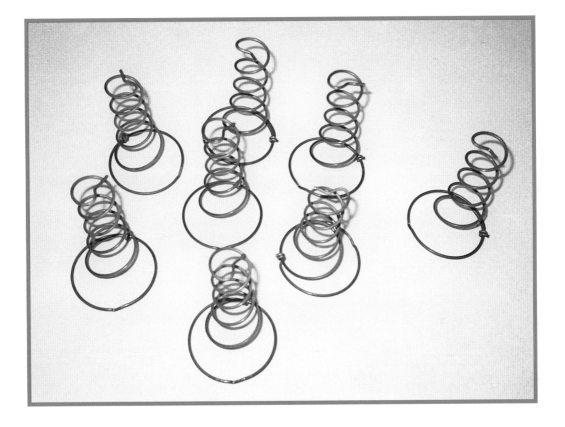

Richard C. Owen Publishers, Inc.
Katonah, New York

Springs are amazing things!

They make things bounce.
They make things spring.

Springs can make things pop up
like the clown in a jack-in-the-box.

Springs can be very big,
like the ones on a train.

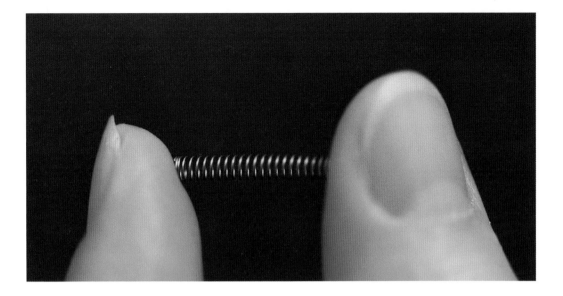

Springs can be very little, like those inside a watch or a computer.

Coil springs are made of wire
that is turned round and round
in a machine called a coiler.

There are different kinds of coil springs.

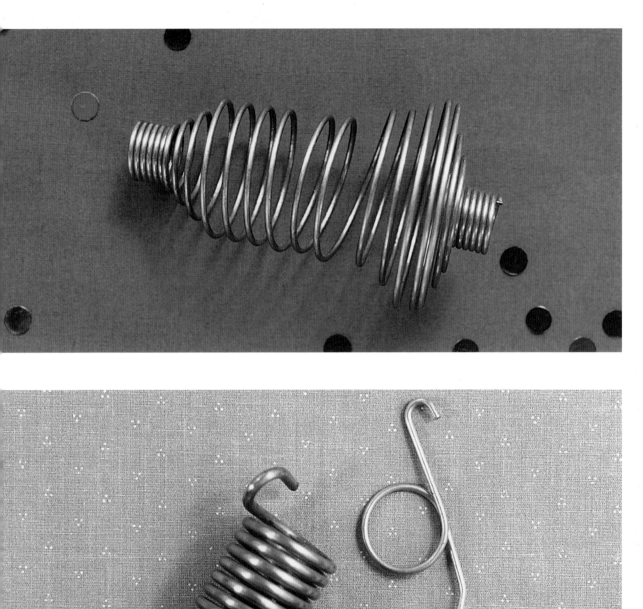

Extension coil springs s t r e t c h.
Screen doors and bouncing rocking horses
have extension springs. So does a Slinky® toy.

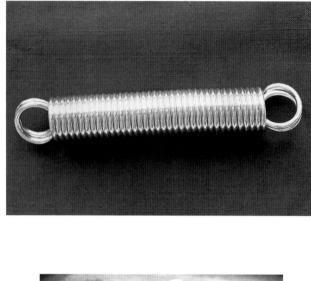

Compression coil springs **squeeze** together.
Bed springs and some toys have compression springs.
You can also find compression springs at playgrounds.

Flat coil springs are found in some clocks.
When you wind the clock, the flat coil spring
turns tighter and tighter from the center out.
As the spring slowly unwinds, the clock ticks.
When it stops ticking, it's time to wind the spring again.

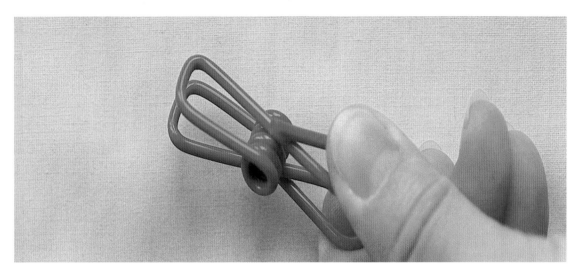

Torsion springs do their work by twisting.
Clothespins, hair clips, and mousetraps
have torsion springs.

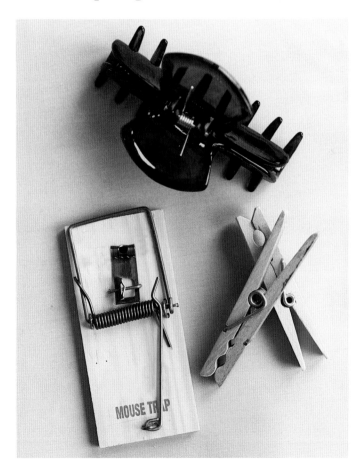

Leaf springs are made of stacks of flat metal strips that bend up and down. Big trucks and boat trailers that carry heavy loads need flat metal springs.

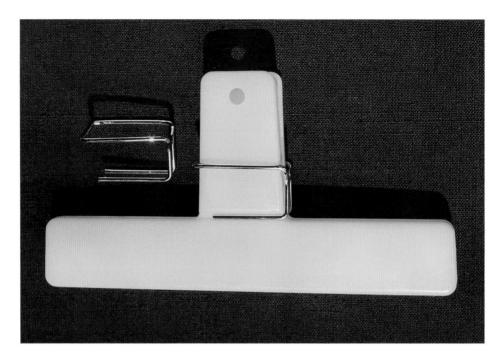

Wire-form springs are bent pieces of wire.
Paper clips are simple wire-form springs.

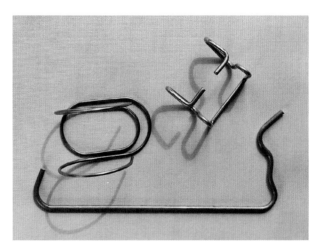

Springs are useful things.
They are amazing things.
They spring up everywhere —
on bicycle seats, on trampolines,
and on pogo sticks, too.

Boing!

Boing

Springs are fun!

Boing!